STRIP CLUB

FOR COUPLES

SHAE'S T-GIRL ADVENTURES
BOOK 3

VICTORIA RUSH

VOLUME 3

SHAE'S T-GIRL ADVENTURES - BOOK 3

COPYRIGHT

For the uninhibited...

1

———

After traveling through most of the Eastern states with our cabaret act, my troupe was ready for a break when our last gig in Pompano Beach finally ended. As our band retreated to the dressing room to take off our stage clothes and makeup, we sighed with relief, knowing we had a week of downtime before the next leg of our tour began to move westward.

"I don't know about you guys," my fellow stage performer, Lola, said while taking off his heavily padded bra. "But I'd be happy if I never have to put on another bustier or pair of Spandex pants ever again. It's too bad we can't perform our act in the *buff*–"

"That would kind of defeat our goal of performing as female *impersonators*," I chuckled, peering down at his dangling package as he pulled off his girdle.

"I dunno," laughed another performer named Raven. "Maybe we could reinvent ourselves as the next *Chippendale's* act."

"Except we don't have the buff *physiques* of those hunks,"

I smiled, glancing at Raven's man-boobs when he took off his fake bra. "We better stick to our theme as drag queens."

"That's easy for *you* to say," my friend Gigi nodded. "You already have a gorgeous figure that doesn't need any covering up."

"All except the part between my *legs*," I grunted, pulling off my tight Spandex briefs and freeing my aching member that was tightly folded between my sweaty labia.

"That's the *best* part," Gigi smiled, his cock twitching while he glanced down at my swollen organ. "I bet we'd make *three* times as much if you were allowed to show that thing during our performances. At least half the women and three-quarters of the guys in our audience have a ladyboy fetish..."

"Other than the fact it's *illegal* to take off our clothes in public," I said.

"Not in Florida," Raven said, tapping on his phone while he performed an internet search. "At least in licensed strip clubs. Why don't we take a break and blow off some steam on the *other* side of the stage tonight? It would be kind of nice to look at some *real* women for a change–"

"A strip club?" I said, wrinkling my brow. "They're just full of leering old men looking for a cheap thrill."

"How's that any different from *our* shows?" Lola laughed.

"At least at our shows, it's mostly gay men just wanting to sing and dance. Those strip clubs are full of weirdos who can barely keep their dick in their pants."

"Come on, Shae," Gigi said, elbowing me playfully in my side. "Let your hair down and relax for a change. We know you like girls as much as guys. And the women at these clubs look like they've stepped straight out of a Playboy centerfold."

"I don't know," I said, frowning as I peered at Gigi in the

mirror. "I just seems so demeaning, watching naked girls perform for money..."

"Nobody's twisting their arm," Raven said. "And you'd be surprised how much these girls can make in a night."

"Are you worried about being able to keep your *own* dick in your pants around all those beautiful women?" Lola teased, peering down at my stiffening tool.

"Hardly," I said, crossing my legs in embarrassment.

"Let's do it then," Gigi said, clasping my hand excitedly. "Maybe we can pick up some new dance moves to incorporate into our routine."

"Or some moves we can work into a few *other* routines," Lola grinned.

After we got changed into our street clothes and piled into two cabs, we headed over to the hottest strip club in town called The Doll House. When we got there, we saw a large neon sign over the front door showing the outline of a naked woman shaking her ass with oversize nipples flashing brightly. There was a long lineup stretching into the parking lot, and as our group joined the back of the line, Lola peered at me with a pained expression.

"It'll take *hours* to get into this place," he said, noticing the line mostly made up of men. "Why don't you talk to the doorman and see if you can work your charms to get us closer to the front of the line?"

"What charms would *those* be?" I said, peering at him with darted eyebrows.

"You could take off your *bra*, for one," he said, glancing at my clingy t-shirt.

"Seriously?" I said, placing my hands on my hips.

"No one else needs to know," Gigi nodded while the rest of my troupe circled around me to provide a degree of privacy. "The bouncer will be happy to have a few more pretty *girls* in the lounge."

I paused for a moment, glancing at the long line-up, then I sighed heavily.

"You guys are going to owe me for this, big time," I grunted, reaching around my back to unclasp my bra and pull it gently over my shoulders.

"The drinks are on us for the rest of the night," Raven smiled, taking my bra and stuffing it in his man-purse.

I walked up the side of the line with the men hooting at my tight ass in my skinny jeans, then I stopped in front of the doorman, puffing out my chest to display the outline of my nipples under the thin t-shirt fabric.

"Can I help you?" he said, darting his eyes downward as he tried to remain composed.

"Yes," I said, passing a crisp fifty-dollar bill discreetly into his hand. "I was wondering if there was anything you could do to help me and my group get into the club a little faster..."

"How many are in your group?" he said, glancing toward the end of the line.

"Ten in total," I said.

"That's a lot to bring in at one time," he said. "We need to obey the capacity limits–"

"I understand," I said, slipping him another fifty-dollar bill. "Maybe you could just move us a little closer toward the front of the line..."

"Is the rest of your group *women*?" he said.

"Not exactly," I smiled. "They're more like *drag queens*..."

"Bring them up here," the doorman sighed, peering down at the bills in his hand. "Just make sure you keep them under control. We have a no-touching policy at our club."

"Of course," I smiled, motioning for my group to join me at the front of the line.

When they skipped up beside me, the doorman shook his head, then he lifted the velvet rope, motioning for us to move smartly ahead while the others at the front of the line grumbled in disapproval.

"That was faster than we *thought*," Lola smiled at me, glancing at my breasts bouncing up and down in my tight-fitting t-shirt. "Did you dazzle him with your high beams?"

"I dazzled him with something a little more pedestrian," I grunted. "Let's just say you guys will be buying me a lot of drinks tonight to make up for my generous donation."

"No worries," Lola grinned as he peered toward the front stage, where two pretty coeds were shaking their naked bodies in front of a cheering crowd. "Something tells me *we'll* be the ones making the rest of the donations tonight..."

2

———

We managed to get a table not too far from the front of the stage, then our group ordered some drinks and settled down to enjoy the show. It felt strange at first, seeing all the naked women prancing around the lounge, including the servers who carried big platters of beer with their bare breasts bouncing mere inches above the foamy heads. But it didn't take long for our focus to return to the stage, where a parade of beautiful women strutted and shimmied to the roar of the crowd while enthusiastic patrons threw a blizzard of bills in their direction.

There was a pole in the middle of the stage where the strippers would go to twirl their bodies and grind their crotches, inviting even more enthusiastic donations from the crowd. I couldn't help laughing when I saw their over-the-top, affected dance moves, each one designed to mimic some form of feigned intercourse while providing teasing glimpses of their bare pussies and asses. I wasn't used to seeing naked women prancing in front of me out of arm's length, with the club's no-touching rule enforced by a band of brawny bouncers, ready to step in if any patron got out of line.

But after a while, I began to enjoy the show while I scrutinized the girl's figures, which were uniformly slender, toned, and perfectly proportioned. Every one of them was tall and slim, with firm, upturned breasts, narrow waists, and legs that went on for miles. And their asses–oh my God, their asses were to *die* for. Firm, tight, round, and shaped like Michelangelo himself had carved them out of a block of marble. There was barely an ounce of fat on any of them, and I wondered where the management team had found them, seemingly hand-plucked from my wildest dreams.

But there was one stripper in particular that I couldn't take my eyes off. With straight red hair falling halfway down her back, her silky tresses undulated over her body as she swiveled her hips from side to side, brushing against her bright pink areolas and clothes-pin-sized nipples with every movement of her body. Whenever she approached the front of the stage, she'd lift each of her legs like a can-can girl, tantalizing us with fleeting glimpses of her shaved vulva and heart-shaped buttocks. It didn't take long for me to begin dripping from just about every orifice of my body while my skinny jeans grew increasingly tight in my crotch from my swelling cock.

When my colleagues began egging her on with loud cheers and throwing a flurry of bills in front of her, she stepped down from the front of the stage and began walking in our direction, locking her eyes on me. I almost had a heart attack when she stopped in front of my chair and turned around, bending over to show me her pretty pucker and her glistening folds. While she squatted over my hips and shimmied her ass mere inches above my throbbing organ, the growing wet spot in my jeans betrayed my barely disguised lust.

"Lap dance, lap dance, lap dance!" my bandmates chanted in unison, throwing even higher-denominated bills at her.

She peered into my eyes as if seeking permission, but I tightened my lips and crossed my legs, signaling that I didn't want her tormenting me any more in front of my friends. The rest of the group booed when she moved to a nearby table, where the next horny onlooker was only too happy to sell his firstborn to have her sit on his bulging crotch and tease him until his eyes crossed in pleasure.

"What the *hell*, Shae?" Lola said, glancing down at the stain in the front of my jeans. "Why didn't you let her sit in your lap? It's obvious that you *wanted* it!"

"It's already uncomfortable enough in these tight jeans," I grunted. "I'm not used to having to pay for it, let alone having to keep my clothes on while a hot coed rubs her body up against me."

"If you'd straightened out your dick before she got here," Raven smiled, peering at the huge bulge in my crotch. "You would have gotten *more* than your money's worth, fully clothed or not. It looks like you could pop off any moment now."

"Possibly," I panted, still trying to catch my breath. "But this is neither the place nor the ambiance for that kind of hook-up. I'm not into public sex, at least not with a bunch of randy old men watching from nearby tables..."

"You could always hire her for a private fling in one of the *back rooms*," Gigi nodded, watching a row of bouncers guarding a bank of closed doors as a string of flushed customers entered and exited on the arm of random strippers.

"Like I said," I grunted. "I've never had to pay for it before, and I'm not about to start now."

There was a change in the music and everyone's attention returned to the stage as the next sexy performer sashayed onto the raised platform.

"What about trying it from the *other* side then?" Lola said. "I bet you'd make a *killing* if you were to go up on the stage and show these horny perverts some of your moves. You're just as hot as any of those strippers, plus you're packing a little extra attraction none of them have. If you showed just a *hint* at what you're hiding under those tight jeans, you'd bring the roof down."

"I'm pretty sure it doesn't work that way," I frowned. "These girls are probably thoroughly screened before they step onto the stage, and they probably have to sign some kind of contract to limit everyone's liability..."

But before I could finish my debate with Lola, the club emcee strolled on the stage, holding up a mic to address the crowd.

"Are you enjoying the show so far tonight?" he bellowed into the mic.

The crowd roared in approval, throwing even more bills onto the stage.

"Well, we've got a special treat for you tonight," he smiled. "Because Saturday nights after midnight are *amateur nights* at The Doll House! Where anybody pretty and courageous enough can strut their stuff and let it all hang out. So who'd like to come up on stage and shake your booty for our appreciative crowd?"

"Woo-hoo!" the room cheered even louder.

"Oh my God, Shae!" Lola grinned at me. "So much for the *contract*. Here's your chance to strut your stuff like we've always dreamed!"

"No way," I huffed, crossing my arms over my chest to signal I wasn't interested.

"Come on, Shae," Raven said. "You don't have to take off all your clothes. You can show as much or as little as you want. You're fucking hot. This crowd will love to see you."

"Plus, you already know how to *perform* in front of a crowd," Gigi smiled. "It's not so different from our cabaret act, where we shake our butts for a bunch of cheering gay men."

"Except I'd be up there all by myself without any props to conceal my private parts..."

"You don't *need* any props to conceal a body like yours," Gigi said. "It'll be fun, and besides–you can keep all the money they throw at you."

"If it's so *lucrative*," I said. "Why don't one of you guys give it a try?"

"Because we don't have a *figure* like yours," Raven said. "This crowd wants T and A, and not the fake, padded type like we use when we're performing."

Fortunately, we were distracted when another loud roar came from the audience as a reluctant coed slowly climbed up the steps onto the stage while her friends cheered her on.

As she began to dance awkwardly to the club music, I flagged down a waitress to order another cocktail. If I was going to consider going up there, I'd need a lot more liquid courage...

$$3$$

———

While one performer after another took the stage to try their turn, I gulped down three more margaritas as I studied their routines. Most of them kept their clothes on, occasionally removing their tops while they shook their hips suggestively for the crowd and slid up and down the big pole to simulate some kind of sex act. After each person returned from the stage, my colleagues pushed me ever more enthusiastically to give it a try. I had to admit that the amateur performances had me intrigued, if only from the awkwardness of their unrehearsed routines.

But one thing kept me interested more than the rest. Standing near the back of the stage during every performance were the rest of the regular strippers, clapping and cheering on the volunteers while they performed their routines. I couldn't take my eyes off the pretty redhead, watching her breasts jiggling while she clapped and smiled, imagining myself sinking my hardening dick into her glistening hole while we rubbed our dripping pussies together. By the time the third amateur performer stepped down, I was almost ready to go up there, if only to get a closer look at her gorgeous body.

"Let's have a big round of applause for our latest performer!" the MC announced, peering out into the audience with his palm over his brow. "I think we have time for one more amateur before we close out the night with a tandem performance from our own group of dancers. Who'd like to come up here and show them how it's done?"

"Come on, Shae!" Lola pleaded. "Here's your big chance. It's now or never. When else are you going to have an opportunity to do your own thing and show off your best features?"

I hesitated for a long moment, glancing at each of my colleagues with a sheepish grin, downing the final drops from my last cocktail.

"Shae, Shae, Shae!" they chanted in unison, egging me to go onto the stage.

When I slowly rose from my chair, they cheered loudly along with the rest of the crowd, and I noticed the pretty redhead nodding at me as she smiled from the back of the stage. While the catchy beat of the Eurythmics song, *Sweet Dreams are Made of This* suddenly filled the room, I slinked up onto the stage, swinging my hips while I crossed my arms over my head, twisting my body like I was in a trance. All eyes from the crowd were on me, but I was only thinking about the sexy redhead while she stared at me from the back of the stage. I dropped to my knees and spread my legs apart, showing off my yoga flexibility, then I splayed them forward and back, gyrating my hips as I pretended to fuck the floor in a scissor position. Then I leaned forward and crawled on my hands and knees toward the front of the stage while everybody threw money at me, arching my back to point my ass in the direction of the pretty redhead.

When that song ended and the dance song *Hot in Herre* by Nelly came over the speakers, I stood up and pulled off my clingy t-shirt, throwing it toward my table where my friends eagerly snatched it up with a whoop. For some reason, it didn't bother me any longer to bare my tits to a crowd of strangers. Whether it was the intoxication from drinking four cocktails or the excitement of knowing the red-headed stripper was watching my every move, I wasn't sure. But one thing was for certain as I wriggled my hips to the suggestive lyrics: my nipples were growing hard as bullets while my dick strained against my tight jeans.

When the seductive song *I'll Make Love to You Tonight* by Boyz II Men came on, I was desperate to rub up against something, and I sashayed over to the chrome pole standing in the middle of the stage, twirling my body around the post and curling my legs around the staff while I humped my hips against it. I was tempted to take off my *pants* also to relieve the pressure from my swelling erection straining against my tight jeans, but I wasn't quite ready to reveal my hidden secret to the whole world. But the more I rubbed my body up and down and swung my hips around the post while the boy-band sang the dripping-hot lyrics, the closer the redhead edged toward me, swinging her hips in rhythm with mine.

Sensing my growing discomfort, when the song *Kiss* by Prince began echoing over the speakers, she stepped out of the shadows, joining me on the other side of the pole while the two of us rubbed our thighs next to one another as we writhed our hips together against the rod. When we squatted down toward the base of the post, we instinctively turned our bodies around, rubbing our asses together against the pole. As we listened to the increasing roar of the crowd, we rolled our bodies closer toward the front of the stage, kneeling on the floor facing one another with my ass pointed in the direction of the crowd while the redhead slowly unbuttoned the front of my jeans. When my swollen cock was finally freed from its confines and it popped upward in my panties, the redhead smiled at me, nodding her head knowingly.

As she began to pull my jeans down over my hips, I rolled onto my back while she slowly pulled off each leg. I placed my arms behind my back and curled my torso upward to conceal my throbbing hard-on angled to one side in my tight panties, then she kneeled over my hips, giving me another fake lap dance while she winked toward the crowd. With a flurry of greenbacks cascading onto the floor all around us, we pretended to fuck one other for a few moments, then I pushed her onto her back as I knelt over her face, rubbing my dripping panties over her cheeks. She reached around the back of my ass and caressed my rosebud, slipping one finger under the seam of my panties and inserting it gently into my slit.

At this point, with my ass still pointing toward the audience and with my panties hanging on by a thread, the crowd still couldn't see my thick cock straining against the front of my panties, angled ten inches over to the side. With the crowd going crazy with mounting desire, and desperate to see the two of us rubbing our naked bodies together, the redhead glanced up at me while squeezing my shaft with one hand and fingering me softly under my panties with her other hand.

"Do you want to want to give them something to *really* cheer about?" she smiled, slowly spreading her legs apart.

"Um–*okay*," I said, peering at her with a worried look.

"It's okay, sweetie," she said. "We're not going to do anything too risqué–just show them what you're hiding under your pretty underwear. You've got something they've never seen on this stage before."

"I don't know," I stammered. "I've never shown my cock in public before..."

"Don't worry," she smiled. "We'll keep it under wraps. We'll just give them something to fantasize about while they fuck you with their imagination and shower us with more money."

"Okay," I said. "What did you have in mind, exactly?"

She flipped me around until I was facing the crowd, then she swung her legs around the back of my hips, crossing her legs in front of my darted panties to conceal my upturned dick. Then she slipped her hands around the sides of my back, running her fingers over my breasts and squeezing them softly while she pinched my nipples from behind. The crowd was now on their feet, cheering us deliriously as they pumped their fists in the air, throwing everything they had left onto the stage to encourage us to go the final step and touch each other directly.

As she continued drifting her hands down the front of my belly, the redhead simultaneously began separating her legs, slowly revealing what I'd been hiding under my panties. When the audience saw that I had a giant poker tenting the front of my panties, they fell silent for a moment in stunned silence, then they erupted into an even louder roar, encouraging the redhead to free my python and stroke it for everyone to see. But instead, she traced the finger of one hand slowly up the length of my throbbing shaft over the veil of my lacy panties, all the way from my soaking slit to my dripping crown. It took everything in my power not to cum all over her hand, but by some miracle, I was somehow able to keep it together, moaning under the music while she brought me to the height of pleasure.

"Save it for *later*, baby," she purred into my ear. "You're holding the Golden Goose there. Don't lay that egg until you're ready to fertilize it. Someone's going to pay you an insane amount of money to have a private room with you."

"I'd rather have a private room with *you*," I groaned in her ear as she caressed my throbbing erection.

"See me after the show," the redhead nodded. "I'll be only too happy to break the no-touching rule with you."

4

———

After the pretty redhead exposed my secret, she moved back toward the rear of the stage, leaving me all alone facing the front of the crowd. While they showered the platform with a blanket of bills and cheered for me to reveal more, I could feel my dick beginning to shrivel from the embarrassment of showing far more than I'd intended. Unsure what to do next, I glanced over at my table, where Lola was motioning for me to move into the crowd, where his rubbing fingers signaled there was a lot more to be made if I mingled directly with the audience.

I hesitated for a moment, frozen in fear, but when the DJ started playing the song *Take a Walk on the Wild Side* by Lou Reed, I began swaying my hips unconsciously to the beat. I stood up and walked over to the edge of the stage, glancing out into the audience to see if I could find anyone I could identify with. When I saw a young couple gazing at me from a table near the side of the stage, I descended the stairs, feeling newly emboldened to extend my act with one last routine. This was my comfort zone–mingling with people one-on-one, while I let them discover my special talents in a more cozy environment.

Even though the bright overhead spotlight followed me as I sashayed toward the couple's table, I blocked out the cheers of the crowd while they egged me on, focusing my attention on the young duo. They appeared to be in their late twenties, well-dressed, and very handsome. The man had perfectly coiffed hair and was wearing an expensive suit, like he was some kind of investment banker. And his pretty date looked like she'd came straight out of a Vogue magazine, wearing a shimmering organza dress and corkscrew-styled hair that cascaded down the front of her plunging V-neck, highlighting her ample bosom and deep cleavage. They ran their eyes up and down my body as I approached their table, keeping their legs crossed over their knees while they twisted the stems of their martini glasses slowly between their fingers, trying to make it look like they were unfazed by my slinky dance moves. But as the suggestive lyrics of the Lou Reed song boomed out over the speakers, I moved closer to the couple, steering over to the girl's side of the table first.

Holly came from Miami, FLA,
Hitch-hiked her way across the USA,
Plucked her eyebrows along the way,
Shaved her legs and then he was a she...

Even though the lyrics weren't an accurate depiction of my gender identity as a female intersex ladyboy, it hinted at my transgender form having both male and female parts, and I intended to use every part of my bisexual arrangement to tease and cajole the seemingly unflappable couple. I walked up next to the cute girl dressed like a flapper from the 20s and leaned over, shaking my breasts in front of her face. She peered down, glancing at my swelling nipples, nodding slightly as a small smile formed on her lips. Then I shifted my hips to the side of her body, sliding my moist panties up and down the side of her bare left arm. Although my dick had almost fully returned to its normal flaccid state, it was still pointing off to the side of my lacy panties, and the girl couldn't help glancing downward while I twitched in my underwear, noticing her distraction.

They said, hey babe, take a walk on the wild side,
I said, Hey, babe, take a walk on the wild side...

While my cock began to grow stiffer and press more firmly against the girl's arm, I felt her muscles starting to twitch as if she wanted to move her hand toward my swelling instrument. As I shimmied my hips harder against her arm and swung my tits directly in front of her face, her eyes widened and her mouth parted when she saw how long my tool had become when it reached its full tumescence. Now that I'd gotten her full attention and disturbed her prim countenance, it was time to get her partner in the game. He'd been examining every inch of my body while I teased his girlfriend, seemingly just as interested in her reaction to my touch as in my response to her growing arousal.

I turned my body away from the girl, then rubbed my ass up and down her tingling arm, making sure she could see that I didn't have any testicles, but a dripping slit in the cleft of my panties instead. Then I wiggled my hips to the rhythm of the music, moving seductively around the front of the table toward the handsome hunk trying to undress me with his eyes.

Candy came from out on the Island, the song lyrics continued,

In the back room she was everybody's darling,
But she never once lost her head,

Even when she was giving head...

The investment banker smiled when I paused in front of him, proudly displaying my throbbing hard-on straining against the thin fabric of my panties. But he kept his legs crossed, holding onto the stem of his martini glass on the table, pretending to be unperturbed. But when I lifted my leg and placed my right heel over his shoulder, his eyes glanced down at the front of my panties, surprised to see a camel-toe where there would normally be of a pair of balls. I noticed some ripples appearing on the surface of his cocktail as his fingers shook ever-so-slightly while he sat rock solid.

I was intrigued to see if I could make any *other* part of his anatomy move while he kept his legs crossed, and as I knelt down slowly in front of his crotch, I raised his top leg and pushed his knees apart. I noticed the front of his trousers tenting slightly, and when I rubbed my breasts over his groin, I felt him growing harder while he pinched the stem of his martini glass harder. I wasn't sure if he was more interested in my boy part or my girl parts, and after starting to get a rise out of him, I stood up and pressed my dick closer to his face while his face flushed and his eyes blinked in growing discomfort.

She said, Hey, babe, take a walk on the wild side,
I said, Hey, Candy, take a walk on the wild side...

By this point, the guy's veins were bulging on the side of his neck, looking like he was about to have an aneurism while he pretending not to be distracted by my ministrations. When the refrain of the song began singing *Doo, do-doo, do-doo, do-do-doo,* I rocked my hips in synchronicity to the beat, pressing the tip of my dripping organ inches away from his trembling mouth. Just when I thought he couldn't take it any longer, his martini class suddenly shattered in his hand, and I pulled away, horrified that he might have cut himself. He picked up a napkin from the table and dabbed it over the palm of his hand, noticing that there was no blood, while two waiters rushed over to the side of the table to clean up the mess and make sure he wasn't hurt.

"I'm sorry," I said, blushing brightly while my dick began to soften in my pants. "I didn't mean to get you so–"

"It's alright," the man smiled, glancing over at his partner. "I enjoyed your attention thoroughly. As did my *wife*, apparently."

I glanced over at the pretty girl who was holding her husband's hand with a concerned look on her face, then she peered up at me with darted eyebrows, making it clear that they'd had enough of my attention for one evening.

"I'm sorry..." I stammered again, slinking back to my table where my colleagues handed me the clothes they'd retrieved from the stage, hastily pulling on my t-shirt and yanking my jeans over my wet panties.

"Well, *that* was exciting," the MC said, retaking the stage to announce the next segment of the show. "But don't worry folks. It appears the only thing the handsome gentleman at the corner table spilled was some of his martini. The next drink is on the house. And speaking of *house*, we're going to close out the night with a few special numbers from our most popular dancers–"

As the Commodores song, *Brick House*, began blaring over the speakers, the pretty redhead stripper strutted back out onto the stage, shaking her ass and swinging her hips to the upbeat music.

Ow, she's a brick house, Lionel Ritchie crooned,
She's mighty-mighty,
Just lettin' it all hang out...
While the redhead smiled and winked at me, I couldn't

help glancing in the direction of the handsome young couple, who looked like they were preparing to leave. As the gentleman scribbled something on a piece of paper and handed it to one of the managers, I was afraid that he might be filing a complaint and possibly suing me for touching him without his full consent. When the manager headed over in my direction and handed me the folded note, my heart skipped a beat as I opened the message. But when I read what the handsome investment banker had written, a *different* part of me started throbbing as a slow smile stretched over my lips.

5

We enjoyed your performance tremendously, the man's note read. *If you'd like to join us for a more private rendezvous, meet us in room twelve in ten minutes.*

After reading his note, I glanced up, noticing that the couple had left their table and disappeared from the lounge. I stopped one of the passing waitresses and asked her where room twelve was, and she pointed toward one of the private rooms guarded by the group of bouncers.

"It looks like your little lap dance with the handsome couple isn't quite finished yet," Lola chuckled, reading my body language to figure out what was going on.

"Maybe not," I smiled, gathering my purse and pushing my chair away from the table. "Will you guys look after my bill while I take care of some other business?"

"Of course," Gigi grinned. "We still need to repay you for getting us into the club. Although something tells me you won't be needing much more financial support after you finish your *next* performance..."

I smiled at my friends and headed toward the ladies'

room to freshen up, then I walked in the direction of the private rooms, stopping in front of the bouncer standing in front of room twelve.

"Excuse me," I said, handing him my note. "I have an invitation to join some of your other guests in this private room–"

"Of course," he nodded, taking the note and placing it in his side pocket while he opened the door halfway. "Enjoy the rest of your evening."

I stepped through the door as the doorman closed it softly behind me, noticing the handsome couple sitting side-by-side on a velvet sofa at the back of the room. The room wasn't as grungy as I expected it to be, with two padded armchairs facing one another opposite the plush sofa, and a small coffee table to hold some drinks.

Spartan, but utilitarian enough to serve its purpose, I smiled to myself.

"We took the liberty of ordering some more drinks," the Wall Street banker said, motioning toward the coffee table where six cocktails were lined up neatly in a row. "Please, take a seat and relax."

Although there was plenty of room on the oversize sofa to join them, I chose to sit in one of the armchairs instead, nodding toward the couple with a smile.

"Thank you," I said, lifting one of the sparkling cocktails with a shaky hand. "Is everything alright with your hand?"

"Not to worry," the man said, raising his left palm. "It was just a nick. Thankfully, it wasn't my dominant hand, so I still have the full use of the *important* one."

"Something tells me you won't be needing it right away," his wife smiled as she winked at me. "Since you have so many *other* ways of tickling your itch tonight."

I was happy to see that she'd lost any animus she might

have previously harbored toward me, but I was unsure what they wanted to do next.

"Um, what did you have in mind, exactly?" I said, pinching my eyebrows. "I've never done anything like this before..."

"What, been with a man and woman at the same time?" the girl grinned.

"No, entertained someone in a setting like this."

"Yes," the man said, reaching into his tailored jacket and pulling out a wad of fifty-dollar bills, placing them on the table next to me. "I guess the first order of business is making sure you're properly *compensated* for your time."

"I'm not that kind of performer," I said, pushing the stack of bills back toward him. "I don't have sex for money."

"Well, you certainly *earned* enough of it while you were strutting your stuff on the *stage*," the man smiled.

"That was unintentional," I said. "I never even bothered to collect any of the money they kept throwing at me."

'I have a feeling somebody's saving it for you," the girl grinned. "You seemed to have made quite an impression on the pretty redhead stripper while you were up there."

"Do you *like* girls?" the man said. "I mean, in that way. Since you seem to have both sets of functioning equipment, we weren't sure of your preferences–"

"I like both genders when the timing is right," I smiled back at them. "Depending on the nature of the company, of course."

"Would you be willing to try something with my wife?" the man said.

"I suppose, depending on what you had in mind..."

"Well, first, I'd just like to *watch* while she takes your clothes off."

"I suppose that could be arranged," I nodded.

"Sweetheart," the man smiled toward his wife while he picked up another cocktail from the side table. "Could you do the honors?"

"It will be my pleasure," she grinned toward me. "As long as you don't spill your load again watching her reveal her hidden charms..."

"It won't be a *martini* I'll be spilling this time, I assure you."

The girl slowly rose up from the sofa and walked around the back of my chair, running her palms over the top of my shoulders and down the front of my chest, squeezing my breasts over the thin fabric of my t-shirt while she pinched my nipples softly.

"Do you *always* go braless?" she said.

"I had to ditch it earlier to distract the attention of another admirer," I nodded.

"No matter," the girl smiled while she cupped my breasts and bounced them gently in her palms. "You hardly need one with these firm melons, anyway. Are they *real*?"

"Yes," I said, slightly irritated by her suggestion that they were fake. "Just like all the *rest* of me."

"Mmm," she smiled, pulling my t-shirt slowly over my shoulders and tossing it on the sofa next to her husband. "So I noticed earlier. That's an impressive thumper you're packing under those skimpy panties. Do you mind if I take a closer look?"

"I suppose not," I said, feeling my dick beginning to harden again and strain against the front of my jeans while she played with my tits.

The girl shifted over to the front of my armchair, then she sank down onto her knees, unbuttoning the top of my pants while sliding the zipper down teasingly.

"You're very good at this, dear," her husband said from

the opposite sofa, raising his martini to his mouth while he tapped his expensive oxfords gently on his knee. "Maybe *you* should have been the one putting on a show earlier and giving us a lap dance."

"Oh, I'll be happy to give a lap dance soon enough," she said, glancing at my swelling erection as she spread open my parted jeans. "Though *which* of you will be the happy recipient, remains to be seen."

"Mmm," the man said, shaking his foot more impatiently. "I can't wait..."

The girl pulled off my sneakers then she grabbed the bottom of each pant leg, dragging my tight jeans down each leg until they were bunched around my ankles. When she saw my aching cock straining against the tight fabric of my lacy panties, she raised herself back up on her knees, pulling the waistband out slowly. My dick popped out of my briefs and swung upwards toward my belly button, slapping loudly against the front of my bare stomach.

"Holy *shit*, Jim," she said, flaring her eyes at my enormous tool. "It's even bigger than I imagined. I thought *you* were pretty well hung, but this girl puts most other men to shame."

"Let me see it," her husband said, uncrossing his legs as he leaned forward to get a closer look at my bobbing erection. "Take off her panties..."

"If you insist," the girl grinned, slowly pulling my panties down over the base of my cock to reveal my dripping slit spilling lubrication onto the faux leather surface of the armchair.

I wasn't sure how many other club patrons had spilled their load on this same chair, but I was glad that it appeared to be clean and unsoiled, for now at least.

"Oh my God," the girl grunted when she saw my stiff

dick pointing up above my dripping pussy. "This is *insane*. I've never imagined anyone this hot in my wildest dreams..."

"That's not what you said to me before we left the table in the main lounge," her husband grinned, reaching down to his crotch to adjust his package in his tightening pants. "Suck her dick. I want to see if she spurts as hard as I do when I come."

"Gladly," the girl said, lowering her head over my bobbing erection while teasing the tip of it with her tongue.

"Mmm," I groaned, watching her flap her tongue around my swelling crown.

"Yes, baby," her husband grunted as he shifted uncomfortably on the sofa. "Suck her cock like you do mine. I want to watch her dick pulsing in your mouth while you drink down her nectar."

"Mm-hmm," his wife nodded, lowering her head a little lower and encircling my glans with her lips.

When she grabbed my shaft with two hands and began stroking me at the same time, I rocked my hips forward, pushing my hard-on deeper into her mouth.

"Fuck yes," her husband said, placing his drink back on the table and leaning back to unbuckle his belt while his dick strained against his pants. "There's something about watching a pretty girl getting her dick sucked that is irresistible. This is way hotter than any porn videos I've seen–"

"I know you like *ladyboys*," his wife nodded, popping her head off my dick to glance in his direction while he pulled his pants down and grasped his reddening tool like he was strangling it with two hands. "I've spied on your browsing history."

"As I have *yours*," he grunted, rocking his dick between his hands while he darted his eyes between my bouncing tits and my bobbing hard-on. "I bet you've never seen one like *this* before."

"Uh-uh," she said, shaking her head while she slid her mouth back over my dripping crown and slamming two fingers into my throbbing tunnel.

"Jesus, that's hot," her husband groaned while gripping his erection tighter and rocking his hips faster in his hands. "Is that a real pussy?"

"Mm-hmm," his wife nodded, unable to take her mouth off my throbbing organ any longer while she hummed and wriggled her hips as she went down on my pole, pushing her fingers deeper into my pussy.

I could feel the nascent pangs of an impending orgasm building up in my hips, and as I watched her pompous husband jerking his hard-on like a teenager with his face flushed a deep shade of red as he teetered on the edge of his own climax, I grabbed the sides of his wife's head and pulled her down harder over my dick. If I was going to be used for their pleasure in the back room of a strip joint, I no longer felt the need for the usual niceties like warning my partner that I was about to come hard in her mouth.

"Fuck, baby," the man grunted, tightening his arm muscles as he began to lift his hips off the sofa while he squeezed his knob harder. "Drink her jizz all the way down your throat. I'm going to come so hard–"

When I saw him spurting all over his expensive suit, I couldn't contain it any longer, and as my semen shot up the length of my pulsating shaft, I held his wife's head down as far as I could over my convulsing cock while I emptied my spunk down her throat and clamped down over her fingers. When both of us finished cumming, she raised her head and gasped for air while she stared at my ruddy instrument, still bobbing and shaking as I spilled the last of my seed out of the tip of my crown.

"Was it as good as you *imagined*?" I smiled down at her as she wiped the last remnants of my cum off the sides of her mouth. "Or at least what you've seen on porn videos?"

"Much better," she panted. "You're way hotter than those trannies on PornHub. Plus, you've got a pussy. I've never seen anyone with both parts before. Nor anyone nearly as pretty as you–"

"Well, I can use those parts in plenty of *other* ways," I grinned. "With both men or women, or even both at the same time. We're just getting started here. Pick your pleasure..."

6

———

"**D**o you want to give it a try, sweetheart?" the girl said, peering over at her husband, whose shrinking dick was beginning to drip all over his hand. "This is your chance to live out one of your fantasies."

"I'm going to need a little time to recover," he said, using a cocktail napkin to wipe the cum off his suit and his hands. "But there's plenty more you can still do with her. I'd love to watch her *fucking* you."

"Yes," his wife smiled as she peered at my cock, still standing straight up and bobbing softly against my stomach. "I've been wanting to do that from the moment I saw her standing next to me with that big thumper straining to get out of her panties."

"How would you like to do it?" I said, glancing down at her plump breasts.

"There are so many ways," she grinned, darting her eyes between my flapping dick and my dripping pussy.

"Well, since your husband is so interested in *watching*, why don't you turn around and sit on my lap so he can take everything in?"

"That would be hot," the girl said, standing up and unbuttoning her dress, then slipping it over her shoulders.

I watched her as she unclasped her bra and threw it on the sofa next to the rest of our clothes, then she wiggled out of her panties, standing in front of me buck-naked with her shaved pussy on eye-level with my face.

"Let me *taste* you first," I said, staring at her glistening sex.

She leaned a little closer, then she lifted her right leg, placing it on top of my left shoulder while her vulva slowly parted, showing the streams of lubrication running down over her tight buttocks.

"Like *this*?" she smiled, echoing the move I'd put on her husband in the main lounge just before he broke his martini glass.

"That'll work," I nodded, grabbing hold of her ass cheeks and pulling her snatch into my face while I lapped up her juices.

"Fuck yes," she groaned as I swiped my tongue up her folds toward her tingling clit. "Suck my pussy while I fuck your face..."

"Mmm," I nodded, peering at her husband with one eye while he hastily removed the rest of his clothes and threw them beside him on the sofa.

His cock was beginning to harden again as he watched me eating his wife's cunt, and I decided to give him a better show to get him back in the mood. I slipped one hand around the back of her ass, then I inserted two fingers into her dripping hole as she arched her back upwards, displaying her splayed pussy for her husband.

"Holy shit, babe," he grunted, taking hold of his rapidly stiffening cock while he locked his eyes on her flexing ass and my hand embedded in her slit. "That's hot as fuck!"

"Which are you enjoying more?" she panted, turning her head to smile at him as he began to jerk his cock faster. "Watching her lick my pussy, or seeing her hard-on bouncing between her legs while she eats me?"

"Both," he grunted. "This is a *million percent* better watching it live..."

"Oh, she's *alive* alright," his wife groaned, grabbing hold of my hair and pulling my face harder toward her dripping pussy. "I haven't had head this good since we first started dating and you put your best moves on me."

"I'm getting plenty of ideas for some *other* moves, watching the two of you go at it," he said, beginning to breathe faster. "I want to come all over your ass–"

"You might want to save that for a little *later*," his wife moaned, rocking her hips harder against my face. "You can't get it up as fast as she can, and you're going to want to save the good stuff for when she turns her attention to you."

"That's a good point," the man said, pulling his hands off his throbbing dick while he took another sip of his cocktail. "Turn around so I can watch her *fucking* you. That'll get me in the mood pretty damn quick."

"It's a shame," his wife said, pulling her hips away from my face, then bending forward to lick her juices off my face as she thrust her tongue into my mouth. "Because I could have come *multiple times* with this gorgeous creature..."

I found it interesting that none of us had bothered to properly introduce one another yet. She'd let it slip that her husband's name was James, but otherwise, we were still acting pretty much like strangers. Very *intimate* strangers, but strangers nonetheless. It didn't bother me really, in fact I preferred it this way, keeping our relationship purely on a physical level, since I knew that I'd likely never see either one of them again after we finished our business in the back room of the strip club. But we'd have to do better than referring to one another as *creatures* or *ladyboys*.

"It's Shae," I said, peering up at her.

"What?" she said, pinching her eyebrows at me.

"My name. It's Shae. It might be easier if we refer to one another by our proper names."

"Is that your *stage* name, or your real name?" the girl said.

"My real name."

"Well, my name's Penelope, but you can call me Penny, for short. And my husband's name is James."

"Pleased to meet you," I said, trying to suppress a laugh when she told me her name.

Talk about stripper names.

"Well, since we're getting to know one another better," Penelope smiled, turning around to rub her ass on my face. "I'd like to acquaint myself more intimately with some *other* parts of your body."

"Be my guest," I grinned, glancing over at her husband, whose dick was bobbing excitedly against his stomach as he watched his wife lower her dripping pussy onto my straight-as-a-chimney erection. "But James might want to put that drink down first. I wouldn't want him to hurt his hand again. He's going to need two of them to properly satisfy both of us when we're done here."

7

As Penelope lowered her pussy onto my hard-on, her husband watched with wide eyes while he squeezed his balls and twitched his other hand next to his bobbing cock, trying his best to keep from shooting off before he had his turn with me. She lowered herself slowly, taking almost a full minute to sink the entire length of my ten-inch-long dick deep into her tunnel. When she'd gone as far as she could, she spread her legs to show James our two pussies nestled next to one another as the base of my thick cock spread her folds apart.

"Holy fuck," James panted, grabbing hold of his dick like he was crushing a beer can. "That's the hottest thing I've ever seen in my life–"

"Even on your *porn* channels?" his wife grinned.

"Even on the porn channels," he nodded as his chest began to glisten in sweat while his body heated up watching us fucking one another.

"Yeah, well this *feels* like nothing I've ever done before," Penny panted, rocking her body up and down my throbbing organ. "You'd never know it was a *ladyboy* fucking you if it wasn't for her dripping all over the chair."

"I'm pretty sure it isn't just *Shae* who's leaking all over the chair," James chuckled, rubbing his thumb over his glistening crown while his eyes focused like laser beams between our joined crotches.

"Is this getting you *wet*?" I said to Penny while I slid my hands over the sides of her ass and teased her vulva as I began to hump her harder over the shaking chair.

"Fuck yes," she grunted, lowering her hand over her swelling clit to stimulate herself while she rocked her ass over my hips. "I haven't been this wet since–well, actually, I can't *ever* remember being this wet."

"I can *tell*," I smiled, lifting my dripping hands up to her breasts while she jilled herself. "I can feel your juices running down over my pussy like a *waterfall*."

She leaned forward a few inches to glance between our legs and I felt her snatch spasming when she saw our bare vulvas rubbing together.

"Oh my God," she gasped. "That is totally *insane*. I never imagined being with a woman this way before..."

"Save that thought," I groaned, thrusting my dick even deeper into her hole. "Because when I'm finished fucking you with my dick, I want to scissor our pussies together and feel you squirting on my *cunny*."

"Not until *I* get a piece of her," James said, rising up from the sofa and walking toward us with his hard-on swinging from side-to-side.

He pushed the other chair off to the side, then he knelt down between our separated legs, pressing his face between our rocking pussies and lapping up our juices all the way from my puckering rosebud to the top of Penny's quivering folds.

"Oh fuck, James," Penny squealed. "Suck my clit while Shae fucks me with her joystick. I want to come all over your face while she squirts inside me."

"Not too *fast*, big boy," I smiled, slowing down my thrusting action. "We need to pace ourselves if you're going to get our money's worth tonight."

"I thought you said you didn't do this for money?" James said, peering up at me.

"I *don't*," I said. "But something tells me *you* paid a pretty penny to reserve this room for this long."

"I did," he said, smiling at his wife. "And she's worth every Benjamin."

"Okay, Benjamin–I mean, *James*," I grinned. "You better get back to work down there to make sure she's properly satisfied."

James nodded his head, then he thrust his face back between his wife's legs, lapping up her juices while she rocked her hips harder against my throbbing cock.

"Fuck, that's hot," I said, feeling my orgasm welling up between my legs while his chiseled jaw spread my labia apart as he sucked his wife's clit.

"Wait!" Penny said, suddenly pushing his face away from her dripping crotch. "I want to make this last a little longer. Suck on *Shae's* pussy for a little while. I want to watch you going down on her. I know that's something you've always dreamed of."

James paused for a moment while he examined my vulva.

"But she doesn't have a *clit*," he said, pinching his eyebrows together.

"My *dick* is my clit," I grinned, peering down at him. "I'll be happy to have you suck it when I'm finished with your wife. But there are some *other* parts down there that are just as sensitive. My asshole, for one..."

James looked up at me, wrinkling his forehead in disgust.

"I've never licked somebody's asshole before," he said. "Isn't that kind of *dirty*?"

"Not if it's been thoroughly washed beforehand," I said. "A proper lady always washes her starfish after every b.m. Your wife's been missing out if you've never treated her to a massage of her rosebud before."

"Okay," he said. "How do I do this exactly?"

"Pretty much the same way you lick her *pearl*," I smiled. "By teasing it with the tip of your tongue and caressing the sensitive areas around the perimeter."

"Like *this*?" he said, lowering his head between my thighs and sticking his tongue between my ass cheeks.

"Yes," I said, raising my hips a few inches off the surface of the chair to give him better access. "Flick your tongue over my starfish. You'll see it doesn't taste nearly as bad as you think."

"Mmm," he nodded, as he pressed his face deeper between my cheeks and probed my perineum with his tongue. "All I can taste is your *pussy juice* dripping down your crack."

"Exactly," I groaned when his wet tongue touched my sphincter. "Lick it harder. That feels so good..."

As James started licking my anus more enthusiastically, I began raising my hips higher while I panted on the back of Penny's neck, feel my climax growing nearer.

"No fair!" she said, grabbing hold of James' hair and pulling his face away from my throbbing pussy. "You're going to make Shae come even before *I've* had a chance! If you're going to lick somebody's asshole to put her over the edge, it better be your wife. Give *me* some of that for a change..."

James glanced a few inches higher, noticing his wife's vulva spasming open and closed, then he peered at her pretty pucker as a big smile spread over his face.

"Yes, baby," he smiled. "I want to feel you coming all over my face when Shae squirts inside you. This is way more fun than I ever imagined..."

When he pressed his face into his wife's cleft and started teasing her butthole with his tongue, she began shaking her hips as she ran her fingers through his hair, bringing my tingling hard-on even closer to the tipping point. Realizing that both of us were teetering on the edge of climax, I slid one hand over her belly to stimulate her swelling clit while I grasped one of her breasts with my other hand.

"Oh fuck..." she gasped, yawning her mouth open as she approached her tipping point. "That feels incredible. I'm going to come, baby. I'm going to come like I've never come before–"

As I felt her body tensing in preparation for a powerful orgasm, I tilted my hips upward, driving my dick all the way to the end of her tunnel. When I felt my cum spraying over her contracting cervix, I pressed my fingers harder against her clit, feeling her entire body convulsing against my hips and my compressed breasts.

"Yes, yes, yes!" she panted, then I felt the tension in her body suddenly released while she flapped her thighs against her husband's buried head, gushing all over his face and his perfectly combed hair. *"Unghhhhhhh..."*

It seemed as if every part of our connected bodies were shaking and convulsing at the same time while we orgasmed together, with James still licking her spasming rosebud until she finally began to relax, easing her vice-grip on his soaking head.

"Oh, my God, Jim," Penny panted as she glanced down at the huge puddle the two of us had created on the slippery armchair. "You have *got* to do that to me more often. That was the hardest and wildest orgasm I've ever experienced."

"Something tells me we're going to learn a lot *more* new ways to satisfy one another before Shae leaves us for the night," he nodded.

"You've got that right," I grinned, peering down at his hard-as-a-rock erection, with his balls nestled up at the base of his throbbing dick like two robin's eggs. "Starting with you. I think that poor pecker of yours needs some relief before your balls explode."

8

———————

"Yeah," James nodded. "I've been holding off for a little longer than I intended..."

"Well, we can do this a number of ways," I smiled. "You can fuck *me*, or I can fuck *you*, or we can both fuck your wife at the same time."

"I'm not into anal sex," he said. "At least not on the receiving end. But maybe that will work for *Penny*, since she enjoyed my licking her butthole so much the last time around."

"Licking it and *plowing* it are two different things," Penny frowned. "But DP in my *pussy*, that's something I've never tried before."

"That does sound interesting," James nodded, his dick suddenly twitching at the idea of rubbing his against mine. "But we might need to move onto the sofa to do that. I'm not sure there's enough room on this little armchair for all of us to fit."

"Yes," Penny said, straightening her legs to lift her dripping pussy off my throbbing cock. "I want to have access to *all* of your parts for this next hook-up."

"We're going to make a mess of that velvet upholstery," James said, glancing at the rivers of fluid spilling off the sides of our chair onto the tiled floor.

I peered over at the rose-colored fabric, noticing it didn't have any stains, and smiled.

"Something tells me they've Scotchgarded that thing five times over," I chuckled. "They probably *steam clean* this place every night, after hours."

"Let's hope so," James said, joining his wife on the sofa with his dick pointing straight up. "Because now we're going to have *three* body parts squirting at the same time."

"Actually, *four*," I smiled. "Depending on which way I'm pointed at the right moment."

"What were you thinking, exactly?" James said. "I mean, you seem to have a lot more experience with this sort of thing than either of us."

"Well," I smiled, glancing over at Penny. "Your wife could sandwich between us while one of us penetrates her from the bottom and the other one lies on top..."

"Or–?" James said, unable to take his eyes off my flapping erection.

"Or you and I could sit with our cocks facing one another while she sits on top of both of us."

"Holy shit!" Penny grunted. "That would be *insane*. Can you imagine feeling her dick rubbing against yours while you both shoot your loads inside me?"

"I've been imagining that ever since she stuck her dick in my face at our table in the main lounge," James smiled.

"Well then, come on over here," I smiled, turning my hips in their direction on the sofa while I padded the cushion beside me. "Have you ever tried *frotting*?"

"What's that?" James said, pinching his eyebrows.

"It's when two guys rub their hard-ons together. Except in this case, you'll be rubbing it against a *ladyboy*."

"Fuck yes," James panted, quickly shifting over to position his hips in front of me as a dribble of precum spilled out the top of his flapping erection.

"Mmm," I purred, squeezing my shaft with two fingers while sliding my slippery crown over the tip of his throbbing organ.

"You're quite a bit larger than me," he grunted, starting down at our two cocks jousting like a pair of fencers.

"I don't think that will matter once you feel your wife's pussy squeezing our two pricks together," I smiled.

"Can I *touch* it first?" he said, widening his eyes as he watched my hard-on slapping against his.

"By all means," I said. "Frotting is even better when you squeeze our two dicks together."

He reached out toward my cock as if it were a snake about to bite him, then he slowly wrapped his fingers around my glans, sliding his hand down the length of my shaft.

"It's magnificent," he said. "I've never felt a cock so thick and long in my life–"

"Exactly how many other cocks have you touched?" I laughed.

"You're the first *ladyboy*," he said. "And you put everyone else to shame."

"Pull our dicks together with your hands," I smiled. "There's nothing like watching two dicks squirting their loads at the same time."

James shifted his hips a few inches closer to me while pressing his balls against my pussy, then he wrapped both of his hands around our joined organs, squeezing them tightly.

"I can barely get my fingers around them," he grunted. "You're huge–"

"You're not so bad yourself," I groaned, rocking my hips upward in his hands, feeling my slippery phallus sliding against his throbbing organ while more pre-cum spilled down both of our shafts.

"Oh my God," he moaned, jerking his hips harder against mine while he watched our two heads popping in and out of the top of his hands. "This feels incredible..."

"Don't come before I get a chance to get in on the action," Penny interrupted, crawling over beside us and placing her hands over James' while the two of them stroked our cocks together. "Don't you want to feel something softer and wetter than just your *hands* stroking your dicks?"

"God, yes," James huffed.

"Which way do you want me to face?" Penny said. "Towards you or Shae?"

James paused for a moment as another dollop of pre-cum spilled out of his helmet and down the sides of Penny's hands.

"Turn around to face Shae this time," he said. "I want to watch the two of you rubbing your tits together when I come inside you."

"Works for me," Penny nodded, smiling in my direction. "I've been dying to rub my tits against you ever since you threw your shirt off the stage."

"And I've been dying to feel *yours* ever since I rubbed my wet panties on your arm," I said.

"Well, we better not waste any more time then," she chuckled, squatting between the two of our bodies while she faced toward me with her pussy dripping like a fountain over our joined cocks.

She leaned forward to kiss me then she slowly lowered her hips downward as James pointed our two cocks into her slit. When she felt both of our tools stretching her opening, she moaned into my mouth, pausing for a moment to allow her body to adjust to the unfamiliar girth entering her cavity.

"Are we hurting you?" I said, peering into her eyes.

"Only a little," she said. "But it's a *good* pain. I've never had two dicks in my pussy at the same time."

"I can come out if you want," I said, tilting my hips downward to pull my cock gently away.

"Don't you *dare*," she said, wrapping her arms around my back and tightening her legs around the back of my ass to keep our hips locked in position. "I don't know when I'm ever going to have a chance to do this again, and I'm sure as hell not going to pass up the opportunity to have sex with my husband and a pretty ladyboy when I've finally got them both where I want them. Let me be the one in charge this time..."

"That's fine with me," I smiled, glancing over her shoulder at James, who looked like he was about to pass out in pleasure. "How about you, James? Are you keeping it together, back there?"

"Oh, they're *together*, alright," he groaned. "It's just that my wife has never squeezed my cock this hard before."

"I'm just getting started, baby," Penny moaned while she slid her pussy further down our connected cocks. "There's a lot more where that came from.

The three of us groaned in unison as she continued sliding her pussy down the length of our shafts until she rested her ass on James' hips.

"All good?" I said, cocking my head to one side.

"*More* than good," she smiled. "Whoever said size doesn't

matter must have had their head up their ass. Because this feels incredible."

"Take your time and enjoy it," I grinned. "If you need to *touch* yourself while you fuck us, go right ahead..."

"Are you kidding me?" Penny said as she began rocking her hips up and down our joined hard-ons. "You're stretching me so much, my clit is rubbing all the way down your shaft. I'm going to squirt all over your pussy when you come inside me."

"Not to mention your husband's *balls*," I grinned as I slid my sweaty breasts against hers while she humped our dicks. "How does that sound for another new technique?"

"It sounds like a dream," Penny huffed, turning her head to the side. "How about *you*, babe? Are you living out your wildest fantasies back there?"

"Fuck, yes," James grunted as he slid his hands around the front of Penny's chest to feel our mashing breasts. "I feel like I've died and gone to heaven."

"Well don't die quite yet," Penny hissed. "Because I want to feel you squirting inside me when I come."

"I'm getting close–" James said, squeezing her tits harder.

"So am I," I grunted, feeling James' tightening balls pressing up against my leaking pussy.

"Let's see if we can do it together at the same time," Penny said, parting her lips as she tilted her head upward in ecstasy.

"Yes," she panted. "Here it comes. *Fuck, fuck, fuckkkkkk!*"

When I felt Penny shaking her body like she was having a seizure and James' hard-on simultaneously pulsing against mine, I lost all remaining control, wrapping my arms around both of their chests while the three of us heaved our bodies together and dug our fingers into each other's asses as we gushed and squirted our combined juices all over the velvet sofa. While we held onto each other's shaking bodies, we turned our faces to one another, kissing passionately, and when we finally finished climaxing, James and I sat still on the drenched sofa, smiling into each other's eyes.

"I never expected to find a stripper like *you* in this joint," he smiled.

"That's good," I said. "Because I always considered myself more of a *diva*. Albeit one who likes to get a rise out of her customers in more ways than one..."

9

———

"So what happens now?" Penny said, resting her hips over mine as our two cocks began to soften in her tight tunnel. "It seems we've done just about every-thing we possibly could, plus I'm pretty sure James won't be able to get it up a third time..."

"I dunno," I smiled. "He said mine wasn't the first hard cock he'd ever seen. Have you ever *sucked* one before?"

"That was a long time ago, in my youth," James said. "I'm not gay–"

"Is it gay if you suck a *ladyboy's* cock?" I smiled. "Especially one who looks like a woman?"

"I never thought about that before," he said as his cock flexed next to mine in his wife's pussy.

"Really?" I said, grinning at Penny. "You've never thought about sucking a ladyboy's cock while watching all those tranny videos?"

"Well, there might have been one or two *cute* ones..." he grinned.

"That's something I've always dreamed about too," Penny said, slowly pulling her hips off our puffy cocks.

"Watching my husband suck another man's cock. We ladies like watching gay sex just as much as you guys dig lesbian porn."

"But Shae's not a man, and I'm not gay–" James protested.

"Even *better*," Penelope grinned. "She's got a cock even bigger than a man's. And like she said, it's not really gay if she looks like a woman."

James paused for a moment as he peered at my glistening tool, tilting forty-five degrees to the side, but still three-quarters hard.

"Come on, James," I grinned. "We both know this is something you've always dreamed about. You already know what it feels like to have a *woman* suck your cock. Here's your chance to try it from the other side..."

"I'm not even sure I could fit that thing inside," he said.

"If I can fit *both* of you in my hole," Penny chuckled. "I'm pretty sure you can fit at least *part* of hers in yours."

"You don't need to take the whole thing inside your mouth," I nodded. "Sucking on just the tip is usually enough to get me off. But I suspect you already know that."

"Let me look at you first," he said, pushing over a few inches as he peered at my bobbing erection. "Why don't you lie on the dry half of the sofa..."

"I think there might be enough room," I said, shifting my body over to the other end of the couch near the opposite armrest.

I lay on my back and rested my head on the armrest, then I spread my legs apart, giving James an unobstructed view of my glistening tits, cock, and pussy.

"My God, you're a piece of art," he gushed, darting his eyes up my body from my painted toenails to my pouting mouth.

"As pretty as the ladyboys on your favorite porn sites?" I smiled.

"Way *prettier*," he said. "Most of them are just *guys* with breast implants. Yours are the real thing."

"Do you want to *touch* them to make sure?" I grinned up at him.

He crawled over toward me, then he knelt over my hips as he leaned forward, cupping my breasts softly in his hands and pinching my nipples gently.

"What do you think?" I smiled. "Are they as real as your wife's?"

"No *shit*," he smiled, squeezing my tits harder. "I'm just not used to seeing them on someone with a giant *hard-on*."

"That's just as real," I grinned. "But you might want to *taste* it, to be certain..."

He glanced down at my organ, watching it drip some leftover cum out of the tip of my crown, then he peered at me with a wrinkled forehead.

"How do you come without any balls?" he said.

I sighed, tired from the common refrain from my lovers. Then I peered up at him with a gentle smile.

"The same way *you* do," I said. "From my prostate gland. Ninety percent of a man's semen is composed of prostatic and seminal fluid. Only a small percentage actually comes from his testicles in the form of sperm."

"Were you *born* this way?" he said, shaking his head in disbelief as he soaked up my sexy ladyboy figure.

"Yes," I nodded. "That's the difference between a trans person and an *intersex* person. Like you said before, the ones you see on your porn videos are mostly men transitioning to be women. I was born as a woman, albeit with one extra part."

"One very *sexy* part," James grinned.

"Go ahead and lick it," I nodded. "Suck me the way *you* like to be sucked."

"Mmm," he nodded, sliding his hips down my torso while he left a trail of semen on my stomach. "Are you sure you don't mind, sweetheart?"

"Are you kidding?" Penny said, pulling up the other chair to have a better look at us while James played with my ladyboy parts. "This is just as much *my* fantasy as yours. I'm going to enjoy myself thoroughly watching you suck her dick."

James pressed my legs slowly apart, then he knelt down in front of my hips, licking up the juices dribbling down the insides of my thighs toward my quivering apex.

"Yes, baby," I moaned. "Tease me slowly and make me beg for it. It's been a while since I've had a blowjob from a man."

"Mmm," James hummed, sliding his head closer to my steaming pussy while he lapped up my juices running down the front of my slit. "You taste incredible..."

"Better than the *other* men you've been with?" I grinned, not believing for a second that his youthful experiments never went as far as he pretended.

"Hmm," he nodded, swiping his tongue up the front of my pussy then all the way up the length of my shaft.

"Fuck yes," I groaned, tilting my head upward. "Lick the underside of my cock. I like watching you suck my dick."

He grabbed hold of my shaft with both hands, then he circled the tip of his tongue around my glans as two more drops of pre-cum spilled out the tip of my dick throbbing in his hands.

"Do you like it when chicks hold your dick with two hands while they suck you?" I grunted, humping my hips upward toward his face.

"He certainly *does*," Penny smiled as she spread her legs apart on the armchair and caressed the insides of her thighs with both hands while she watched her husband go down on me. "At least with *this* chick."

"Suck my cock while I watch your wife play with herself," I grunted, pulling his head further down my shaft. "You're not the *only* one who likes a good show."

James resisted my pressure for a moment, then he tightened his lips around my flaring crown, sucking me harder while he pumped his hands faster up and down my shaft.

"Do you like watching your hubby suck my dick?" I said to Penny as she slipped two fingers into her dripping tunnel and began circling her clit with her other hand.

"Fuck yes," she groaned. "This is the best show I've seen him put on in a long time."

"I'm glad to know I'm not the *only* one putting on a show tonight," I grunted as he bobbed his head over my swelling dick. "Are you enjoying this as much as we are, James?"

"Mm-hmm," he nodded while he increased the pace of his bobbing and jerking.

"Put your fingers inside my pussy," I told him. "I'm going to watch your wife jill herself at the same time."

"Yes," Penny huffed as a deep flush began to spread over her bouncing tits. "Feel her pussy tightening around your fingers when she comes..."

"Are you beginning to feel *your* pussy tighten?" I said, noticing her buttock muscles contracting as she neared orgasm.

"Yes," Penny panted. "Make Shae come with your fingers and your mouth at the same time. Curl your fingers inside her pussy the way you do with me..."

"Mm-hmm," James moaned louder over my cock as he felt my body tensing.

"I'm going to come soon, James," I said, wanting to give him some advance warning in case he'd never actually experienced someone cumming inside his mouth. "You're an awesome cocksucker."

"Oh my God," Penny suddenly hissed, lifting her hips over the edge of the armchair. "I can't hold it any longer. Ssssst–*kah!*"

When I saw her gushing all over her hands and the back of James' curled torso, I couldn't hold it any longer, and when I realized that James was going to let me come in his mouth, I grabbed the back of his head, thrusting my cock deeper into his cavity while I shot one powerful blast of cum after another down his throat, rocking my hips wildly against his head. By the time Penny and I had finished squirting and spraying all over his body, his hair was thoroughly drenched, looking like he'd just come out of the shower.

"Holy crap, baby," Penny panted, smiling at her husband when he lifted his dripping lips off my swollen organ. "If you'd told me you like ladyboys this much, I would have given you one for a present, long ago."

"It's never too late to dip your toe in the water," I smiled. "Or take a dive in the deep end."

10

———

Suddenly, there was a soft tap on the door, and the three of us peered at one another with a puzzled expression.

"Have we overstayed our welcome in the back room?" I chuckled, glancing at James.

"I paid to have the use of the room for the entire evening," he nodded, getting up to see who was at the door.

When he inched it open, I noticed the pretty redhead stripper from the stage tilting her head to the side, peering at me with a concerned expression.

"Is everything okay back here?" she said. "I got a little worried when you didn't come to see me after the show..."

"Yes," I smiled, glancing at Penny, sitting naked beside me. "We're having a lovely time getting to know one another better. Would you care to *join* us?"

"I don't want to interrupt if you're in the middle of something–"

"We were just finishing up," I smiled. "But I think there might be room for one more. What do you say, James and Penny–do you mind if we make it a *foursome*?"

"Not at all," James grinned, motioning for the redhead to come in as he closed the door softly behind her.

"It looks like you've been busy back here," the redhead smiled, glancing at the soaked armchairs and the pile of crumpled clothes lying of the sofa.

"Yes," I said, laying our clothes over the wet cushions to invite her to join me on the sofa while James and Penny made themselves comfortable on the two facing chairs. "We never had a chance to properly introduce ourselves. My name's Shae, and these are my new friends, James and Penny."

"Pleased to meet you," the redhead said. "My name's Autumn."

"We enjoyed your show earlier in the evening," James said, crossing his legs to hide his dripping dick. "*Both* of yours."

"Although it was never properly *consummated*," Penny smiled, crossing her legs sexily like Sharon Stone in the movie Basic Instinct. "Would you care to finish your show in this back room?"

"I'm not sure," Autumn said, glancing down at my semi-flaccid dick. "Are you still able to rise to the occasion?"

I peered at her bald pussy as she draped one leg over my knee and smiled at her as my cock slowly began to slide up the side of her thigh.

"For you," I grinned. "I could come a *country mile*."

"Mmm," she purred, slipping her hand between my legs and drifting her fingers over my bobbing pole. "You look even *hotter* with your panties off. I never really had a chance to feel the rest of your body..."

"Nor me with *yours*," I said.

"Well, it looks like you're no longer afraid to show all your pretty parts," Autumn said.

"I have a smaller audience this time."

Autumn glanced in the direction of James and Penny, who smiled back at her while they nodded their heads softly.

"Don't let *us* stop you," James smiled. "We're just happy to watch this time."

Autumn peered back at me, then she pressed my body down onto the sofa until I was lying flat with my dick pointing straight up. She crawled down to the opposite end of the couch and knelt over my feet, massaging them softly while she lowered her pussy above my toes. When I felt her warm gusset touch my digits, I groaned unconsciously, twitching my cock toward my stomach as two drops of cum cascaded over my belly button.

"Mmmm," she moaned when the toes of my right foot entered her slit.

The sight of her fucking my foot with her gorgeous figure was unlike anything I'd ever seen before, and I couldn't help grabbing my dick with two hands and pumping it rapidly while I watched her writhe over my appendage.

"Jesus..." James groaned at the same time, parting his knees as his dick popped up between his legs. 'You guys really should have finished that show on the stage. The audience would have *mortgaged their houses* to watch you two do that completely in the buff."

"If it weren't for the no-touching policy.," Autumn smiled.

"Well, that policy doesn't apply *here*," he said, grabbing hold of his hard-on while his wife lifted her knees over the edge of her armchair and slid her fingers over her mound.

"No," Autumn smiled, leaning forward to caress the top

of my shins with her breasts while she drenched my toes with her dripping pussy. "It suppose it doesn't."

I reached down, trying to stroke her beautiful hair, but she remained just out of reach while she teased me with her tits and pussy. I flexed my right foot, desperate to feel her sex any way I could, but she lifted her hips off my toes then dragged her pussy up the length of my trembling legs, coating them with her glistening juices. When she got next to my hips, she placed her palms atop my thighs, then she slid her hands around the base of my dripping tool, probing the edges of my quivering pussy with the tips of her thumbs.

"I'm guessing you've had practice doing this sort of thing before," I panted as I stared into her green eyes.

"Not with anyone as pretty as you," she smiled.

"Or as *hard*," I grinned, removing my hands from my cock to display it flapping inches away from her face.

"Mmm, yes," she purred, massaging the area around my mound harder while I dripped like a waterfall down the front of my vulva and the crack of my ass. "You're even bigger than I thought."

"And wetter," I grunted, rocking my hips faster, practically begging her to touch me.

"What a pretty *pussy* you have," she said, blowing softly on my vulva as she kissed her way up toward my quivering quim.

When her mouth touched my sex, she slipped her tongue inside my slit, then she placed her hands under my thighs, pressing them forward until my entire perineum was exposed for her view. She paused for a moment, enjoying the sight of my parted pussy and my puckering sphincter, then she flattened her tongue and swiped it all the way from the top of my butt crack to the base of my flapping hard-on while I grunted like a pig.

"Are you taking *notes*, James?" Penny groaned as she played with her clit while watching us.

"Definitely," he grunted, jackhammering his cock in his clenching fists. "I've got *plenty* of plans for that part of your body once I get home with you."

While James and Penny were enjoying the show, I peered up at Autumn with beseeching eyes.

"Autumn," I panted, staring at her with a flushed face. "I need you to touch me–*higher*."

She pulled back for a brief moment and glanced at me with a raised eyebrow, then she peered down at my bobbing hard-on, dripping rivulets of pre-cum down the sides of my shaft.

"Here?" she grinned, inserting the tip of her middle finger gently into my spasming slit.

"Higher..." I grunted, rocking my hips until my dick swung from side-to-side like a flagpole in a hurricane.

"Here?" she said, sliding her finger a few inches higher toward the top of my folds.

"Oh God, *higher*," I groaned, staring at her with pleading eyes.

She paused for a second, smiling at the tortured look on my face, then she leaned a few inches further forward, sandwiching my throbbing organ between her perfect breasts and mashing them together while she remained motionless.

"Here?" she smiled, feeling my cum rolling down over her tits while she grinned up at me.

"Yes," I moaned. "I want to feel you on my cock. *All* of you..."

"Well, I'm not sure I can give it *all* of my attention," she grinned as she slithered up the front of my stomach, leaving a trail of cum up my abdomen. "But I might be able to give it just enough to satisfy *both* of our needs."

"Fuck yes," I shuddered as she rolled her tits over mine, moving her body higher until her wet pussy slid over the tip of my pole, snapping it backwards as it slapped against the back of her ass.

When her face became level with mine, she leaned forward to kiss me, and I thrust my tongue deep into her mouth while I tilted my hips upward and slid my throbbing cock between the crack of her ass, feeling her juices rolling over my belly and down the insides of my thighs.

"Please, baby," I moaned into her mouth while I slapped my dick against the back of her ass. "Please fuck me. I need to feel your pussy on my cock..."

"Yes," James panted from his armchair a few feet away. "We need to see it almost as much as she does. This is the sexiest show either one of us have ever seen here. There's going to be a huge tip for you later–"

"Perhaps not quite as big as *this* one," Autumn smiled, peering into my eyes as she lifted her hips off my quivering stomach and perched her pussy over my flaring crown. When she finally lowered her dripping vulva over my organ, all four of us grunted in simultaneous ecstasy.

"Autumn," I grunted, looking up at her with a twisted face. "I'm sorry, but I can't hold it any longer. You've already taken me to the peak of my pleasure. I'm going to come, baby. I'm going to come in your sweet, warm pussy."

"Yes, baby," Autumn purred in my ear while she kissed me around the edges of my parted mouth. "Come for me, Shae. I want to feel you pulsing inside me."

"Oh God," I panted in her ear, feeling my floodgates open. *"Unghhhh..."*

While I felt my dick exploding inside her tunnel, I could vaguely hear the sound of James and Penny moaning and grunting beside me, but I was so focused on the incredible sensation of having Autumn hold me while I came inside her sweet pussy, that everything else faded away for what felt like an eternity. When I finally finished shaking underneath her, she cradled my head in her hands, kissing me softly while she squeezed her pussy against my pulsing pole, milking the last remaining drops out of my spent prostate gland.

"Thank you for coming down to see me," I whispered into her ear. "I hadn't planned on spending this much time in the private room."

"I can see why you did," she smiled, twisting her head to peer at James and Penny, who'd slumped down in their chairs with their legs parted far apart, dripping their juices over the front of their seats. "That's a pretty hot couple you've been busy satisfying back here."

"But I still haven't satisfied *you*," I said, realizing that I'd come far too fast to give her a chance to climax with me. "What can I do to please you?"

"Well, if you're interested in getting your *friends* back in on the action," she smiled. "I've got an idea how we can satisfy *all* of us at the same time..."

"**I** don't think I've got any juice left in the tank," James panted, overhearing our conversation.

"That's quite alright," Autumn said, glancing at his shriveled dick. "As far as I can tell, you seem to prefer watching anyhow. But something tells me your *wife* still has a few laps left in her..."

"I could come all *night* playing with the two of you," Penny nodded, sitting upright in her chair as she pinched her swollen nipples. "What did you have in mind, exactly?"

"Have you tried DP yet?" Autumn smiled.

"If you mean two pricks in my pussy at the same time, yes," she said. "But how would that work with three women and only one cock?"

"I meant double *pussy*," Autumn grinned. "Two pussies rubbing against one cock. You should try it sometime. It's almost as good as two cocks in one pussy."

"That does sound hot," Penny nodded, twisting her nipples harder. "But what about Shae? Has *she* got any juice left in the tank?"

"Maybe not," I chuckled, feeling my dick throbbing

inside Autumn's tight pussy. "But my *crankshaft* is still working."

"Let's see if we can get her back in the mood with *two* drivers behind the wheel," Autumn smiled, lifting her hips off my dripping tool as it leaned wearily to one side. "Why don't you come over here and kneel next to me, facing in the other direction? Most of the important stuff is on the *outside*, anyway. If we rub our clits against her leaning tower, maybe we can breathe some new life into it."

"Mmm," Penny nodded, raising up off her armchair and walking over toward the sofa, pausing in front of the two of us while she tilted her backside toward my face. "That's not the *only* thing I plan on rubbing up against while I'm humping her cock."

She climbed on top of me facing Autumn, then she swung her left leg over the side of my hips, nestling her moist crotch over the base of my flagging erection. Autumn pulled it up between their bare mounds, then she shifted her hips further forward until they'd wedged my dick between their bodies.

"I'm not sure you're going to be able to do *anything* with this wet noodle," she smiled at me. "Are you sure your heart is still in the game?"

"The *spirit* is willing," I said, staring down at Penny's pretty ass perched over my abdomen. "I'm just not sure my flesh is able..."

"Maybe it just needs a little extra *massage*," Autumn said, reaching down between her legs and caressing the top of my dripping crown with the tips of her fingers.

"Mmm," I purred, feeling some blood returning to my pole. "That feels good..."

"I think she might need a little more help getting her back in the mood," Autumn said to Penny. "Maybe two *tongues* might be a better way to get things started than two pussies."

"Sounds good to me," Penny nodded, shifting her hips backwards toward my face while she leaned forward, licking the front of my dripping organ like an ice cream cone.

I glanced at her bare ass splayed in front of my face, then I tilted my head slightly upward, tickling her anus with the tip of my tongue.

"Unghh," she grunted as my cock began to swell from the women's combined ministrations.

"*Fuck*, James," Penny panted to her husband. "You might not like it up the ass, but *I* sure as hell do. At least with a soft tongue. You're going to be spending a lot more time with your head between my legs after this."

"My pleasure, sweetheart," James grunted, starting to play with his hardening cock again as he watched me diddling his wife.

"It's starting to *work*," Autumn nodded, noticing my tool beginning to thicken and rise higher over my crotch. "I'm not sure if it's from our licking her sex or her licking yours, but try to keep it going a little longer until she's completely hard."

"I'm in no hurry to stop, believe me," Penny groaned, pushing her ass harder into my face.

The harder my dick became, the more enthusiastically they licked it, concentrating their attention on my swelllng bulb while they flicked their tongues around the edges and lapped up my slippery juices.

"Is that cum from the *last* time you shot your load, or from *this* time?" Autumn smiled at me. "Because it sure looks like you're getting back in the mood pretty quickly"

"A little bit of *both*, I suspect. You better start grinding your pussies if you want to catch some while you can."

"What do you say, Penny?" Autumn said. "Do you want to rub a *different* part of your anatomy against Shae while she's up for the occasion?"

"If you insist," Penny said, reluctantly pulling away from me and sliding her body forward to rub her tits against Autumn's as the two women peered at each other, inches apart. "As long as I can get a new kind of tongue action."

They swung their legs around the back of each other's hips, then Autumn grabbed hold of Penny's head and thrust her tongue deep into her mouth.

"Fuck yes," I groaned when I felt their wet pussies rocking against my throbbing organ as they tribbed their pussies together.

"Do you *like* that, Shae?" Autumn grinned, peering over Penny's shoulder.. "Are we beginning to refuel your tank?"

"I'm not sure about the *tank*," I shuddered. "But the *pistons* are sure as hell firing on all cylinders again."

"Good," Autumn panted. "Because you're taking me from zero to sixty pretty damn fast."

"Me too," Penny groaned, glancing over at her husband with one eye. "I was already pretty close to the edge after Shae licked my ass. How about you, James? Have you got your motor revving again?"

"Oh, it's revving alright," he smiled, swinging his erection from side to side as he rolled his hips watching Penny and Autumn grinding their pussies together on my dripping tool.

"Do you want to get in on this too?" Penny said. "This might be your last chance to get a lap dance with two strippers."

"I'd love to," he said, darting his eyes over our joined bodies. "But I wouldn't know where to slip into the action."

"What about *DT?*" Penny smiled, glancing at Autumn with a raised eyebrow.

"DT?" James said, peering at his wife quizzically.

"Double *tits,*" she said. "You can stick your dick between our breasts while we're mashing our bodies together. I bet four will feel *twice* as good as two."

"Holy shit," he said, jumping off his chair and hopping over to the edge of the sofa. "This night just keeps getting better all the time."

When James poked his erection between our slippery breasts, getting a tit-fucking like he never dreamed, the four of us started moaning together in unison, growing closer to one final, collective climax. I had no idea which bouncer might still be guarding our door, but whoever it was, he was definitely getting an earful from our combined grunts and moans while we jerked, rubbed, and slapped our bodies together.

"Are you ready, Shae?" Autumn said, glancing at me as her face began to flush a deep shade of red.

"I'm always ready," I smiled, feeling another climax building up beneath the base of my cock.

"What about *you*, James?" Penny huffed, glancing at her husband, who was watching his dick disappearing in and out of the two women's bouncing breasts.

"Fuck yes," he panted. "I'm going to cream all over your melons..."

"You better make it good," she grunted. "Because I'm about to have the biggest climax I've had all night. *Oh fuckkkk...*"

As the four of us began to shake our bodies together in simultaneous climax, I shot my last load of the night between Penny's and Autumn quivering bellies while James spurted over their tits and the two women gushed all over my dripping crotch. It was the perfect way to end an evening of surprising twists and turns, but I hoped it wouldn't be the last time I'd have a chance to see Autumn again. As we put our wet clothes on and prepared to leave the club for the night, I pulled a card out of my purse and handed it to the pretty stripper.

"If you ever want to see a *different* kind of show," I smiled. "Come see me at the Lips Revue. I perform there three times a week."

"*Lips*, hmm?" she grinned, peering at the iconic image of my club with the pursed woman's mouth. "I like the sound of that..."

～

R eady for more ladyboy chills and thrills? Read the next volume in Shae's T-Girl Adventures: The Boys' Room. Buy direct and save at victoriarusherotica.com. Or download from your favorite online bookstore here: retailer links.

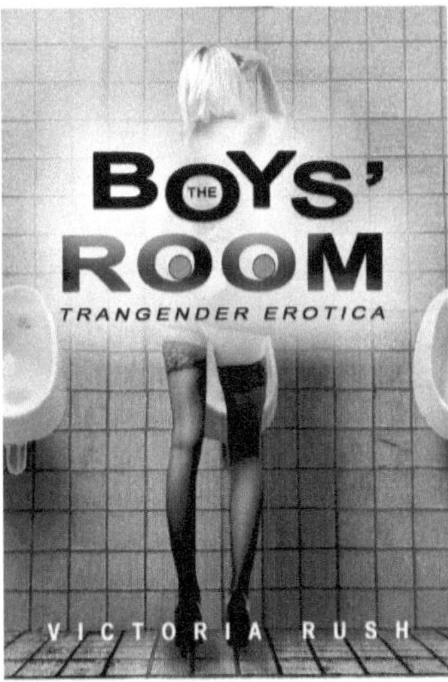

There's a reason public washrooms are sometimes called the 'head'...

ALSO BY VICTORIA RUSH

Adult Fairytales:

The Enchanted Forest: An Erotic Fairytale

The Land of Giants: An Erotic Fairytale

The Dragon's Lair: An Erotic Fairytale

Witch's Brew: An Erotic Fairytale

The Mage's Spell: An Erotic Fairytale

The Mermaid Lagoon: An Erotic Fairytale

The Coven: An Erotic Fairytale

Rapunzel: An Erotic Fairytale

The Seven Dwarfs: An Erotic Fairytale

The Land of Mutants: An Erotic Fairytale

The Erotic Temple: A Sexy Fairytale (Coming Soon)

Erotica Themed Bundles:

Voyeur: Lesbian Erotica Bundle

Public Affairs: A Lesbian Anthology

Futa Fantasies: The Ladyboy Collection

Threesomes: The Lesbian Collection

Threesomes - Volume 2: The Lesbian Collection

First Time: A Lesbian Anthology

Hedonism: An Erotic Anthology

Switch Hitters: Bisexual Erotica

Taboo Erotica: The Lesbian Series

BDSM: The Lesbian Collection

Party Games: The Erotic Collection

Party Games 2: The Erotic Collection

All Girl 1: Lesbian Erotica Bundle

All Girl 2: Lesbian Erotica Bundle

All Girl 3: Lesbian Erotica Bundle

All Girl 4: Lesbian Erotica Bundle

Erotic Fairytale Bundles:

Clover's Fantasy Adventures: Books 1 - 5

Clover's Fantasy Adventures: Books 6 - 10

Erotic Fantasy:

Pirate's Bounty: A Time Travel Adventure

Wild West: A Time Travel Adventure

Private Riley: A Time Travel Adventure

Cleopatra's Secret: A Time Travel Adventure

Bounty Hunter 2125: A Time Travel Adventure

Ninja Assassin: A Time Travel Adventure

The 300: A Time Travel Adventure

Arabian Nights: An Erotic Fairytale (coming soon...)

Steamy Time Travel Bundles:

Riley's Time Travel Adventures: Books 1 - 5

Lesbian Erotica:

The Dinner Party: Lesbian Voyeur Erotica

The Darkroom: Bisexual Voyeur Erotica

Naked Yoga: Lesbian Transgender Erotica

Nude Cruise: Bisexual Voyeur Erotica

Rush Hour: Taboo Public Sex

The Girl Next Door: First Time Lesbian Erotic Romance

Girls' Camp: Lesbian Group Sex

Wet Dream: Ladyboy Fantasy Erotica

The Convent: Taboo Sex with a Nun

Sex Robot: A Dream Sex Machine

The Personal Trainer: Getting Pumped at the Gym

The Dominatrix: BDSM Lesbian Domination

Webcam Chat: Lesbian Online Sex

Paint Me: A Kinky Bodypainting Workshop

The Toy Party: Girls Sharing Sex Toys

The Costume Party: Strapping One On

Swedish Sauna: Lesbian Group Sex

The Therapist: Taboo Lesbian Erotica

Elevator Shaft: Bisexual Threesomes Erotica

Ladyboy: Lesbian Transgender Erotica

Peep Show: Lesbian Voyeur Erotica

The Dare: Public Sex Erotica

Maid Service: Lesbian Threesomes Erotica

The Hitchhiker: First Time Lesbian Erotica

The Housesitter: Spycam Lesbian Erotica

The Spa: Lesbian Group Orgy

Parlor Games: Blindfold Sex Party

The Exchange Student: First Time Lesbian Erotica

The Hostel: Bisexual Group Erotica

The Harem: Lesbian Erotic Romance

The Orient Express: Lesbian Voyeur Erotica

The First Lady: A Forbidden Lesbian Erotic Romance

The Slave: Lesbian BDSM Erotica

The Masseuse: Lesbian Sensuous Erotica

Too Close for Comfort: Lesbian Forbidden Erotica

Naked Twister: A Wild Party Game

Lexi: The Sex App (Lesbian Fantasy Erotica)

Call Girl: Lesbian Bisexual Threesomes Erotica

Circle Jill: Lesbian Masturbation Workshop

The Viewing Room: Masturbation Voyeur Erotica

Spin the Bottle: A Kinky Party Game

The Hair Salon: Lesbian Voyeur Erotica

Tribadism 1: Girls Only Sex Workshop

Tribadism 2: The Art of Scissoring

Tribadism 3: Threeway Hookups

The Kiss: A Game of Oral Sex

Pledge Week: Sorority Sisters

Carny Games 1: A Wild Sex Party

Carny Games 2: A Kinky Sex Party

Carny Games 3: An Erotic Sex Party

Dreamscape: An Artificial Reality Game

Glory Hole: Guess Who's On the Other Side

Joy Ride: A Late Night Erotic Bus Trip

The Blind Girl: An Erotic Romance(Coming Soon)

Lesbian Erotica Bundles:

Jade's Erotic Adventures: Books 1 - 5

Jade's Erotic Adventures: Books 6 - 10

Jade's Erotic Adventures: Books 11 - 15

Jade's Erotic Adventures: Books 16 - 20

Jade's Erotic Adventures: Books 21 - 25

Jade's Erotic Adventures: Books 26 - 30

Jade's Erotic Adventures: Books 31 - 35

Jade's Erotic Adventures: Books 36 - 40

Jade's Erotic Adventures: Books 41 - 45

Jade's Erotic Adventures: Books 46 - 50

Fifty Shades of Jade: Superbundle

Standalone Stories:

The Polynesian Girl: A Lesbian EroticRomance